SCAREDY CATS

For Alex

Find out more about the Scaredy Cats at Shoo's fabulous website: www.shoo-rayner.co.uk

ORCHARD BOOKS
96 Leonard Street, London EC2A 4XD
Orchard Books Australia
32/45-51 Huntley Street, Alexandria, NSW 2015
First published in Great Britain in 2005
First paperback edition 2005
Copyright © Shoo Rayner 2005
The right of Shoo Rayner to be identified as the author
and illustrator of this work has been asserted by him in
accordance with the Copyright, Designs, and Patents Act, 1988.
A CIP catalogue record for this book is available
from the British Library.
ISBN 1 84362 447 8 (hardback)
ISBN 1 84362 746 9 (paperback)
1 3 5 7 9 10 8 6 4 2 (hardback)
3 5 7 9 10 8 6 4 2 (paperback)
Printed in Great Britain

Catnapped!

Shoo Rayner

ORCHARD BOOKS

Tinker crept out of the sculptor's studio where he lived. He froze on the path, hypnotised by the pale, glowing eyes that stared down at him.

An icy wind blew. The air filled
with a tooth-grating clash of steel.

The moon slid behind a cloud. The glowing eyes faded away and Tinker saw that they were only holes in a huge sculpture. The sound was the wind blowing through its metal bones.

Tinker ran to the secret circle, where he told the other eight members of the Secret Society of Scaredy Cats what had happened.

"I-I-I really thought the sculpture was alive!" he puffed.

The other cats nodded. They all
knew that the wind could make
strange noises.

"It was weird," Tinker explained.
"I was really hypnotised by the
moonlight in the sculpture's eyes."

"You're lucky it was only a
sculpture..." said Kipling, their leader.

Silence fell upon the secret circle. Kipling's eyes narrowed into slits. He was ready to tell a story. The story they had all come to hear.

Kipling looked them all in the eye and began. "My Uncle Bingo lived near a most extraordinary place."

It was a dark and mysterious wood.
Towering yew trees leaned over
the paths.

Their twisted trunks looked like ancient people, frozen in time. No grass grew, only shiny-leaved ferns.

It was easy to lose yourself in the wood. The paths had a magical way of going round in circles. If it weren't for the old man at the gatehouse, no one would have ever escaped!

His name was Napper. He looked as
old and twisted as the trees he cared
for. His huge eyes were a shade of
ocean blue. Looking into them was
like drowning in the wild, open sea.

Something else made the park special...the statues of cats and dogs and other small pets.

The statues were so realistic that people came from all over the world to see them. You could often hear them say, "I thought I saw a statue move!"

Bingo liked to hunt at the edge of
the wood, but one day he strayed
further than usual and found himself
on a mysterious path.

It was a puzzle! Whichever way he
went, the path returned him to the
same place! The trees made a wall on
either side. There were no gaps.

There was no way to get off the path...he couldn't even find the place where he had joined it!

As he wandered round the wood, Bingo had the creepy feeling that the statues were watching him.

They looked so real. He felt their
eyes follow him as he walked past.

Then Bingo realised he *was* being
watched. He felt the power of those
dazzling blue eyes.

It was Napper, gazing at Bingo from
his gatehouse. His big eyes seemed to
say, "You're not getting out this way!"

Tiredness crept over Bingo as he
desperately searched for another exit.
He collapsed under a spreading fern
and soon fell into a deep, heavy sleep.

When he woke, the sky had grown dark and the moon was throwing mysterious patchwork shadows on the trees. How long had he been asleep?

As he stretched himself awake,
Bingo realised that he was not alone.
His body went rigid with fear.

He was surrounded by statues! They stared at him with cold, unfeeling eyes. Slowly, they shuffled towards him, licking their dry lips, murmuring and sighing.

He backed away from them, but
they crowded the path behind him,
closing off his means of escape.

There was only one way he could go. The path was like a river, sweeping him along its dangerous course that lead, at length, to the gatehouse.

Napper towered above Bingo!
His wild eyes were aglow in the
moonlight. In an instant, Bingo was
gripped by their magnetic powers.
He was helpless.

"So," Napper smiled. "You've come to join us for a little catnap in my wood, have you?" He spoke in a sleepy, dreamy voice.

"Can you feel it yet?" he asked.
"Your body is turning to stone.
Starting at the tip of your tail, the
feeling will slowly creep all over you."

Bingo tried to swish his tail. It didn't move!

As Napper continued speaking, Bingo felt his body grow stiff.

Bingo wanted to see what was happening, but he couldn't tear his gaze away from those piercing blue eyes.

The hypnotic words became a murmur. Bingo was losing control of his body. He was losing his spirit too.

The end was coming. Soon he would be just another statue in the wood. Now he understood why the statues looked so real. They *were* real.

But Bingo was a strong-willed cat.
From deep within, he summoned the
power to tear his eyes away from
Napper's. It was only for a second,
but that was all it took.

He hadn't turned to stone yet!

With every scrap of energy he could muster, Bingo sprang at Napper. His sharp claws slashed fiercely at those terrible eyes.

Napper screamed with pain and fury.

Dazed and terrified, Bingo
scrambled over the gate and ran
for his life.

The sound of a stampede told him that the stone animals were after him.

Bingo was soon exhausted.
The living statues were catching up
with him, snapping at his heels.

Bingo tripped and fell. He felt them
crowding around him. This time there
really was no escape.

He opened his eyes, fearing the worst... Real, furry animals stared at him, surprised by their new-found freedom. Bingo had broken Napper's sleeping spell.

Yelping with joy, they disappeared
into the night, in search of their old
owners. Bingo lay on the grass,
blinking in the streetlight.

In the distance, Napper staggered along the road, his eyes closed and powerless. He sobbed, "My little friends...my little, furry friends...come back...come back!"

Kipling had finished his story.
From far away, the sculptor's voice
called across the night.

"Tinker! Tinker! Time to come home."

"I'd better be off!" said Tinker,
warily.

"Mind how you go," said Kipling.
"And...be careful which path you take!"

CATS

Shoo Rayner

❏ Frankatstein	1 84362 729 9	£3.99
❏ Foggy Moggy Inn	1 84362 730 2	£3.99
❏ Catula	1 84362 731 0	£3.99
❏ Catkin Farm	1 84362 732 9	£3.99
❏ Bluebeard's Cat	1 84362 733 7	£3.99
❏ The Killer Catflap	1 84362 744 2	£3.99
❏ Dr Catkyll and Mr Hyde	1 84362 745 0	£3.99
❏ Catnapped	1 84362 746 9	£3.99

Little HORRORS

❏ The Swamp Man	1 84121 646 1	£3.99
❏ The Pumpkin Man	1 84121 644 5	£3.99
❏ The Spider Man	1 84121 648 8	£3.99
❏ The Sand Man	1 84121 650 X	£3.99
❏ The Shadow Man	1 84362 021 X	£3.99
❏ The Bone Man	1 84362 010 3	£3.99
❏ The Snow Man	1 84362 009 X	£3.99
❏ The Bogey Man	1 84362 011 1	£3.99

These books are available from all good bookshops,
or can be ordered direct from the publisher:
Orchard Books, PO BOX 29, Douglas IM99 1BQ
Credit card orders please telephone 01624 836000 or fax 01624 837033
or e-mail: bookshop@enterprise.net for details.

To order please quote title, author and ISBN and your full name and address.
Cheques and postal orders should be made payable to 'Bookpost plc'.
Postage and packing is FREE within the UK
(overseas customers should add £1.00 per book).

Prices and availability are subject to change.